Cabbage Patch Kids
A Year Full of Fun!

Published by Modern Publishing, a division of Unisystems, Inc., New York, New York 10022

Printed in the U.S.A.

1 3 5 7 9 10 8 6 4 2

Background photograph credits
Cover: © 1998 Andre Gallant/The Image Bank; p. 1: © H. Armstrong Roberts; p. 3: © 1998 Andre Gallant/The Image Bank; p. 4: © H. Armstrong Roberts; p. 5: © 1997 Marcia Lynn Bockol; pp. 6-7: © H. Armstrong Roberts; p. 8: © H. Armstrong Roberts; p. 9: © 1997 Comstock; p. 10: Brett Patterson/Westlight; p. 11: Bill Ross/Westlight; pp. 12-13: © H. Armstrong Roberts; p. 14: ©1998 David W. Hamilton/The Image Bank; p. 15: © H. Armstrong Roberts; p. 16: © H. Armstrong Roberts; p. 17: © H. Armstrong Roberts; pp. 18-19: © H. Armstrong Roberts; p. 20: © Camerique/H. Armstrong Roberts; p. 21: © 1998 Giuliano Colliva/The Image Bank; p. 22: © 1998 Patti McConville/The Image Bank; p. 23: Nick Rains/Westlight; p. 24: © 1998 Chuck Kuhn/The Image Bank.

Meet the Cabbage Patch Kids® gang!

Mary Beth

Megan

Justin

Norma Jean

Nick

A.J.

Myles

Vernon

Melonie

Michiko

Travis

Barry

Prissy

Shereena

Billy

Missy

Can you find them in this book?

It's windy in **WINTER!** It's cold, and it snows!
So bundle on up, from your head to your toes!

Get ready for parties, and lots of great fun . . .
Cards to be opened, and ribbons undone.

Or stay up real late greeting Baby New Year,
With a tall glass of milk to toast heath and good cheer!

And down at the ice pond, it's time to go skate,
Around and around in a big figure-eight.

And if you are lucky, there's ice-fishing too,
But don't stay too long or your lips will turn blue!

Next: Valentine's Day, to warm up our hearts . . .
Just watch out for Cupid and all his love-darts!

For a last winter venture, a last winter fling,
Just ski down the mountain, right into . . .

SPRING!

Take just enough time for a quick bite to eat.
Then it's down to the ballfield— your team can't be beat!

And keep your eyes peeled for a bunny or chick.
To find bright-colored eggs, you'll have to be quick!

Relax in the garden, where the berries are red,
Or play with the butterflies all day instead.

The sunlight is perfect at spring photo shoots,
For the shutterbug 'Kid™ up-and-comer.
But while you are busy just snapping away,
Along will come, suddenly . . .

SUMMER!
Up and down sidewalks is a perfect bike ride,
If there's lots of foot traffic, just move to one side!

Dust off that sail-board, and catch the next wave!
In the sun, wind, and spray, you've got to be brave.

Even staying at home, with your waterwings on,
You can take a quick dip out on your front lawn!

Hike through the meadow and climb mountains tall!
When the weather gets cooler, it's finally . . . FALL!

Leaves crunch underfoot, there's a snap in the air,
It's just not the time for your feet to be bare!

In a special new costume, it's trick-or-treat time,
With black cats, and goblins, and a dark midnight chime!

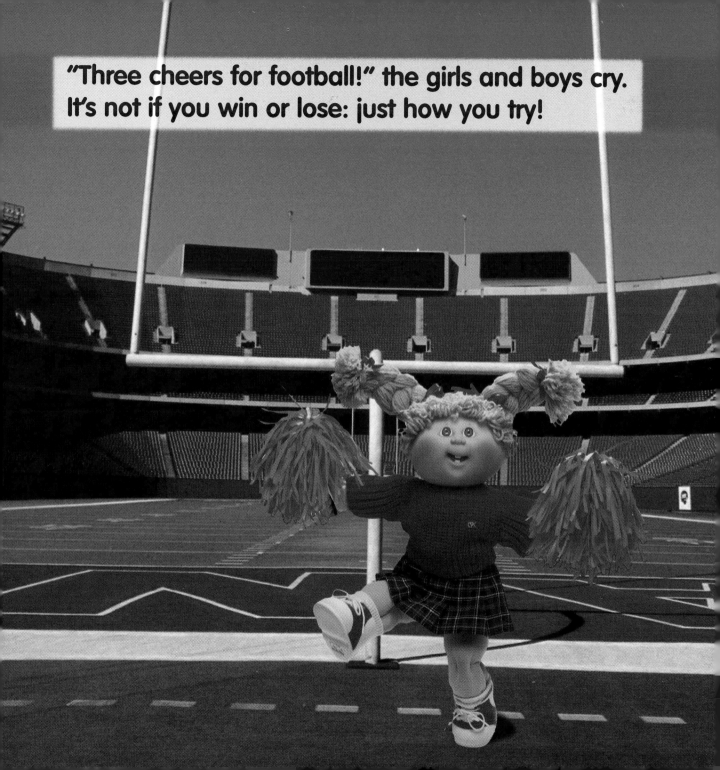

"Three cheers for football!" the girls and boys cry.
It's not if you win or lose: just how you try!

There's lots to talk over with friends on the phone.
You'll find plenty to do even hanging at home!

All the year 'round, think of great things to do,
Some busy, some quiet . . . some old and some new.

Play a fast game of soccer! Hurry up! Run!
There's no time to waste . . .
The whole year's full of FUN!